The Elevator Family
Hits the Road

You might enjoy these other titles
by Douglas Evans:

The Elevator Family	*Delacorte Press*
The Elevator Family Takes a Hike	*WT Melon*
The Classroom at the End of the Hall	*Front Street*
Math Rash and Other Classroom Tales	*Front Street*
Mouth Moths, More Classroom Tales	*Front Street*
Apple Island, or the Truth About Teachers	*Front Street*
MVP: Magellan Voyage Project	*Front Street*

WT Melon
www.wtmelon.com
"good stories: good tunes"

The Elevator Family Hits the Road

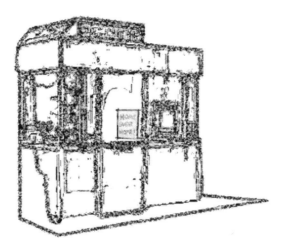

Douglas Evans

WT Melon
wtmelon.com
2014

ISBN: 0615686710
ISBN-13: 978-0615686714

For My Family

The Wilson family's green compact car rolled along the winding highway. With his large belly pressed against the steering wheel, Walter Wilson stuck his elbow out the window. He threw back his head and sang,

"There was a man who had a dog,
And Bingo was his name-o!
B-I-N-G-O! B-I-N-G-O! B-I-N-G-O!

And Bingo was his name-o!"

In the back seat, the ten-year old twins, Winslow and Whitney Wilson, groaned.

"That's the twelfth time you sang Bingo today," said Winslow.

"We've played I-Spy six times, and the license plate game ten times," said Whitney.

Winona Wilson sat in the passenger seat beside her husband. A buttery sun melting into the road ahead reminded her of the hour. "Time to find a place to stay tonight," she said. She studied the highway map of Illinois. "This road is about to cross a wide blue line."

"Fantabulous" said Winslow. "That's the Mississippi River. M-i-s-s-i-s-s-i-p-p-i."

"I'm for staying on the banks of the Mississippi tonight," said Whitney. "I-p-p-i-s-s-i-s-s-i-m."

"The Mighty Missisip! Father of Waters! The Big Muddy!" said Walter. "Old Man River!"

Minutes later, the Wilson's car passed a sign:

Toll Plaza Ahead

"Toll Plaza!" said Winona. "That sounds like a

pleasant place to stay."

"I once read the book *Eloise at the Plaza*," said Whitney. "The Plaza was a fancy hotel."

"The *Plaaawza!*" said Winslow.

Soon the green compact drove onto a long iron bridge, spanning the wide, chocolate-colored Mississippi River. Ahead four small cabins stood side-by-side across the right-hand lanes of the highway. Each had large windows on three sides and a wide door on the other. A single sunroof covered all four cabins.

Walter parked beside the cabin closest to the river. Stenciled on the front was a big red 4. A zebra-striped gate crossed the lane in front of the Wilson's car.

"Splendid! A gem of a place," Walter said. "Never seen anything like this Toll Plaza. Little cabins standing right on the highway."

"And the price is very affordable," said Winona. "The sign says *Toll Five Dollars*."

"And we're not by the Mississippi, we're over it," said Winslow. "Fantabulous!"

Whitney spotted a person sitting in each of the other

three cabins. "The rest of the toll cabins are taken," she said. "We're lucky cabin four is vacant."

"All in favor of staying in this Toll Plaza cabin tonight say *one-Mississippi*," said Walter.

"*One-Mississippi!*" all chorused.

The family piled out of the car. They stood on a narrow cement patio in front of the little cabin.

At that moment, a red sports car drove up to the cabin next door. This cabin had a big 3 on front. The driver handed something to the woman inside and continued across the bridge.

Shortly afterward, a blue mini-van stopped at Toll 3. Two children in back pressed their noses against the window and made faces at the Wilsons. The family waved, as the van sped on.

"Very friendly people on this bridge," said Walter. "Only the best."

"And this Toll Plaza seems popular," said Winona. "People are being turned away every minute."

The Wilsons walked up to the vacant cabin.

Whitney opened the bottom half of the side door

and then the top half. "Very cool!" she said. "A Dutch door!"

"There's even a telephone, a stool, and a fan inside," said Winslow. "Fantabulous!"

"The interior is bright and clean," said Winona.

"And the view of the river is spectacular," said Walter. "What a vista!"

"This even beats the small windmill we stayed in last night," said Winslow. "The green carpet was comfortable, and all evening people tried putting golf balls around us."

"The night before, I liked staying in that long narrow cabin next to a baseball field," said Whitney. "It had one wall missing, so we could watch the baseball game."

"Each inning a team came to visit us," said Walter.

"So let's unpack the compact, family," said Winona. "With a little decorating, this toll cabin will fit our family just fine."

Out the western window, a golden sun was dipping below the far side of the bridge.

Walter put one arm around his wife and the other

around the twins. "Only the best for this family," he said. "And these are the best accommodations west of the Mississippi, east of the Mississippi, and *above* the Mississippi."

The Wilsons hung their hammocks inside the little cabin, Walter a red one, Winona a blue one, Whitney a yellow one, and Winslow a green one. Winona placed the camp stove and cooking pans on the back shelf, while the twins stuffed their pajamas and paperback books in the drawer beneath it.

For a final touch, Walter hung an embroidered sampler by the Dutch door. It read:

HOME SWEAT HOME.

"A family tradition," he said. "Home Sweat Home hangs wherever the Wilsons stay."

"How long ago did the twins stitch that sign?" asked Winona.

Whitney rolled her eyes. "We were in second grade," she said.

"Spelling wasn't our best subject," said Winslow.

Back on the cement patio, the twins set up lawn chairs and Winona the aluminum camp table. For his part, Walter assembled the barbecue grill.

"Hot dogs for dinner," he said. "Hot diggity dog! We're having hot dogs!"

Walter dumped charcoal into the grill and sprinkled on ample lighter fluid. A Greyhound bus was passing through the Toll Plaza when he tossed in a match. *Phooom!* A five-foot flame shot into the air.

"Stop by for dinner," Walter called to the wide-eyed passengers staring out the bus windows. "Always room for guests wherever the Wilsons stay."

As Walter grilled the hot dogs, Winona spread a checkered tablecloth on the table. From a large wicker picnic basket she unpacked plastic plates and silverware. "What a lovely place for a picnic," she said. "No bugs and plenty of scenery."

Meanwhile inside Toll 4, the twins studied three light switches by the Dutch door.

"Eenie-meenie-minie-moe," said Winslow, and he flipped the left-hand switch.

A fluorescent light flickered on overhead.

"My turn," said Winona, and she flipped the middle switch.

This time a neon OPEN sign attached to the sunroof glowed green.

"Open?" she said. "What could that mean?"

Together the twins flipped the third switch, and the zebra-striped gate crossing the lane swung up.

"Fantabulous," said Winona. "Now we can have visitors like the other cabins."

Sure enough, at that moment a black Ford drove up

to the Dutch door. The driver wore a Saint Louis Cardinals baseball hat on his head and a scowl on his face.

Walter waved his barbecue fork. "Greetings, friend!"

"Lovely evening, isn't it?" said Winona.

The man held out a five-dollar bill to the twins inside the cabin and scowled some more.

Whitney shook her head. "Sorry, sir, keep your money," she said. "This toll is already taken."

The driver smiled for the first time. "Hey, thanks, honey," he said, and drove off with the wave of his hand.

Seconds later, an eighteen-wheeler truck pulled up to the door. The twins pumped their fists up and down, and the truck's horn blasted. *Burrrrrp!*

"Care to join us for dinner?" Walter asked the driver.

"Kind of you to ask," he replied. "But I have two-hundred more miles to drive this evening." He tried handing Whitney five dollars, but she also refused him.

"Come and get it, family!" Walter announced, as the semi pulled away. "Dinner is ready! Hot diggity-dog!

We're having hot dogs!"

"Whitney, close the gate and turn off that **OPEN** sign," said Winona. "Everyone who passes seems to think our cabin is available."

Each Wilson loaded a hot dog onto a bun.

Winona spread mustard on her wiener, while the twins spread catsup on theirs. Walter, however, doused his hot dog with both mustard *and* catsup. He held up the orangey creation for his family to admire.

"This is what I call a *mussed-up* hot dog," he said.

While the Wilsons ate, the sky turned purple. Lights from the city across the river twinkled, matching the twinkling lights of the countless fireflies on the near bank. Cars swished by on the bridge, and the Mississippi River flowed lazily below.

"Marshmallow time," said Winona. "Let's have a contest. Whoever toasts the best-looking marshmallow-- totally golden-brown and perfectly symmetric--is the winner."

Winslow retrieved the marshmallow forks from the car trunk, and each Wilson speared a marshmallow. They held them over the glowing barbecue coals. Almost at once, Walter's marshmallow burst into flames. He waved his fork back and forth until the flame went out. Too late. On the end of the fork hung a bubbly, black glob.

"Not the prettiest marshmallow in the world," he said. "But it's just how I like to eat them."

As he spoke, a siren wailed. Racing toward the Toll Plaza in the opposite direction, blue lights flashing, was a black police motorcycle.

"A visitor from the west side of the bridge," said

Winona.

"Excellent!" said Walter. "Guests are always welcome."

The motorcycle roared past the Toll Plaza, made a sharp U-turn, and stopped next to the Wilsons on the cement island. A short, brawny policeman wearing a leather jacket swung his legs over the bike seat and strutted up to the grill. The sticker on his white helmet read:

MISSOURI STATE POLICE

"Well, this beats all," he said. "When a toll taker called to tell me a family had moved onto the bridge, I thought she was pulling my leg."

"We just checked in," Walter told him. "We're the Wilsons, the new toll takers."

"Toll Four is just the kind of place our family prefers to stay in, small and tidy," said Winona. "We're a tight-knit family."

The policeman pulled a spiral notebook from his back pocket. "Well, lady, I have half a mind to throw you in a place that's even smaller and tidier than this one. It also has iron bars to keep you there."

At that moment another siren blared. Soon a white police car pulled up to the zebra-striped gate. Words on the side read:

ILLINOIS STATE POLICE

From the squad car stepped a tall, lanky policeman. He pushed back the brim of his hat with a thumb and addressed the first officer. "What do we have here, Fred?"

The Illinois policeman waved his notebook. "Now we've been through this before, Ed," he said. "This Toll Plaza is in my state, so I'm in charge here."

He pointed to a sign riveted to the side of the bridge: WELCOME TO MISSOURI.

"Well, that's not how we see it in Illinois, Fred," said the second policeman. "The sign on the other end of the bridge says WELCOME TO ILLINOIS. So officially we're in my state."

"Drat!" Walter suddenly shouted. His second marshmallow had set fire.

The two policemen paused to watch Walter whip his long fork in the air as if he were a sword fighter. Then they resumed arguing.

"Ed, this is the great state of Missouri," said the motorcycle cop. "And since this family is breaking Missouri trespassing laws, I'm going to give them a fistful of tickets and move them out."

"Sorry, Fred," the Illinois policeman said. "This family is roasting marshmallows in my state. So I'll say if they stay or not."

The men might have gone on bickering if Whitney and Winslow hadn't held their marshmallow forks toward them. On the end were two toasted marshmallows with golden-brown sides.

"Have one," the twins said together.

"Well, will you look at that?" said Fred. "I haven't seen such finely toasted marshmallows in all my days camping." He plucked the marshmallow off Winslow's fork.

"That's a beauty, young lady," Ed said to Whitney. "A real work of art." And he pulled off hers.

Together the policemen placed the marshmallows on their tongues.

"Deeeeeelicious," said Fred. "Best marshmallow in

the state of Missouri."

Ed licked a thread of marshmallow off his lip. "Nothing like it in the entire state of Illinois."

The pair looked toward the Wilsons still standing around the glowing grill.

"Tell you what, Ed," said Fred, flipping his ticket book closed. "It's getting late. I guess this matter can wait until tomorrow when I can talk to the Missouri state judge."

"Yep, we've been arguing about this Toll Plaza for ten years now, Fred," said Ed. "No chance of getting anything settled tonight. I say we call it a day, and I'll talk to the Illinois judge in the morning."

Fred mounted his motorcycle and revved up the motor. "Enjoy your night in Missouri, Wilsons," he called out. And he roared off across the bridge.

"See you tomorrow, folks," said Ed, climbing into his squad car. "Hope you like it here in Illinois."

As the second officer sped away, Walter raised another flaming marshmallow from the grill. "Not the prettiest thing in the world," he said. "But it's just how I like eating them. Just fine with me."

*B*eep! *Beep! Screeeeech! Varoom! Honk! Honk!*

The sound of traffic woke the Wilsons before sunrise the next morning.

Walter sat up in his hammock, scratching his belly. Headlights flashed on the glass. The top half of the Dutch door was open, and a man dressed in a gray uniform and a gray hat sat on the stool. The zebra-striped gate was up, and the OPEN sign glowed. One by one cars stopped by the door. Each driver handed the man some money.

"Mornin', thanks. Mornin', thank you," the man said.

"Greetings, sir," Walter called out. "Visitors are always welcome in Toll 4."

The man turned. "Mornin' back to you," he said. "Charlene next door told me a family was sleeping in here. Most excitin' thing that's happened on this bridge in years. Another day; another handful of dollars. I hope I didn't disturb you."

Winona sat up, yawning. "You must be here to take over our cabin," she said. "We didn't know checkout time was this early."

"Yep, I've been takin' tolls on this bridge for over forty years," said the man. "By the way, my name's Huckleberry."

"We're the Wilsons," said Walter. "I'm Walter and this is Winona. Next comes Whitney, and that's Winslow still snoozing in the far hammock."

Whitney sat up. "Did you say your name is Huckleberry?" she asked. "Like the boy in Mark Twain's novel *The Adventures of Huckleberry Finn?*"

"Yep, that's who I was named after, on account I was born on the banks of the Mississippi like old Huck Finn himself," said the man. He took a five-dollar bill from a man in a blue pickup. "Fact is, I was raised on the Mississippi and went to school on the Mississippi. I wed on the Mississippi and worked here above the Mississippi all my life. I've traveled up and down the Mississippi, but have never traveled east or west of this river for more than a mile." Huckleberry accepted a ten-dollar bill from a man in a cement truck and handed him change.

"Huckleberry Finn ran away and floated down the river," said Winona.

"Yep, often I sit here starin' down at the Mississippi and think about Huck Finn fishin' on his raft," said the man. "Even from up here I can see catfish jumpin' in the water. Yep, if I had one wish, I'd wish to be down there right now, fishin' on the river like old Huck Finn."

As the man collected another five-dollar bill, Walter

looked toward Winona and nodded. Winona nodded toward the twins, and the twins nodded toward Walter.

"Well, Huck, quit wishing and go fishing," Walter said. "If you'd let us, we'd like to take Toll Four for another day."

"We'd love to stay longer here in Illinois or Missouri or whatever state we're in," said Winona.

Huckleberry leaped off his stool. "You wouldn't mind taking over for me?" he said. "I mean, it's not the most excitin' place to be. Another day; another handful of dollars. And I gotta warn you, some drivers can be downright rude, especially during Rush Hour when it can get mighty busy."

"This bridge couldn't get busier than the small red room we stayed in during our trip to England," said Whitney.

"People dropped by every few minutes to use our telephone," said Winslow.

Huckleberry flipped a switch, and the zebra-striped gate closed. "Then I reckon' number four is all yours," he said. "I hate to leave you right before the mornin' rush, but now's best time for catchin' catfish."

"We even have a fishing pole you can use," said Walter. He tumbled out of his hammock and led Huck to the compact. From the trunk he took a bamboo pole and a straw hat. He also handed him a few marshmallows.

"Marshmallows are the best bait for catching catfish I've ever used," he said.

Huckleberry replaced his gray hat with the straw one. He untucked his shirt and removed his shoes and socks. Waving to the Wilsons with the fishing pole, he took off along the sidewalk toward the Illinois side.

"Yep, Huck, is goin' fishin'," he called out. "I'm off to catch some catfish in the Old Mississippi."

At that moment, the sun peered above the Illinois horizon. Golden sunbeams spread onto the bridge, lighting up the Toll Plaza.

Walter stepped over to the bridge guardrail to enjoy the view. "Rise and shine, everyone," he said. "We've had a lucky break. We get to stay at the Toll Plaza for another day."

W alter stood on the cement patio doing his

morning toe-touching exercises. "One-Mississippi, two-Mississippi, three-Mississippi," he said, bending over as far as he could "Four-Mississippi, five-Mississippi."

At that moment a newspaper van drove up next door. Walter raised a finger, and the driver tossed a newspaper onto the patio.

"Excellent service at this Toll Plaza," Walter said, returning to the little cabin. "How about pancakes for breakfast."

Winona started the camp stove on the back shelf, while Walter mixed a batch of pancake batter.

"Today my pancakes will be in the shape of different states in the United States," he said, greasing up the frying pan. "Before you can eat the pancake, you must guess what state."

Winona, Winslow, and Whitney sat around the aluminum table. Walter placed the first pancake on Winona's plate. She studied it a moment before guessing, "New York!"

"Correct!" said Walter. "You may eat, my dear."

"You're a pancake artist, Walter," said Winona, as she poured syrup on the spot where New York City would be.

Whitney received the next pancake. "South Carolina!" she guessed correctly, and she, too, began eating.

Winslow, however, frowned at the pancake Walter gave him. It was smaller than the end of his fork. "Rhode Island," he grumbled. "Come on, dad. I'm starved."

"Then make way for the biggest pancake this side of the Mississippi," Walter said, and he placed a pancake on Winslow's plate so large that it hung over the sides.

"Alaska!" Winslow said.

While the Wilsons ate breakfast, more cars appeared on the bridge. They formed long lines outside the other three toll cabins.

"This must be what Huckleberry called Rush Hour," said Winslow.

"Odd to have an hour just for rushing," said Whitney.

"What's the rush?" said Walter.

"Why don't we open our gate and find out where everyone is rushing to?" said Winona.

She entered the cabin and flipped the gate switch. The moment the zebra-striped gate opened, a red pickup truck stopped at the Dutch door. The driver, a bearded man in blue overalls, handed Winona a ten-dollar bill.

"Lovely morning, isn't it?" Winona said.

"I wish I could enjoy it," said the driver. "But I have seven lawns to mow this morning. I'd like some change."

"A change can be very rewarding," said Winona. "That's why my family likes to travel." She handed the man back the bill. "And you can keep this. All the tolls are taken today."

"Well, thanks, lady," said the driver. "That starts my day out pleasantly for a change."

After breakfast, Walter read the newspaper, the twins read paperbacks, and Winona remained at the door, chatting with drivers. She talked with a large man in a green Plymouth, followed by a small lady in a red Mustang. Next came a teenager in a Volkswagen van and a silver-haired woman driving a blue Honda. Each driver tried handing Winona five dollars. Of course, she always refused taking the money.

"Walter, I'm meeting the most interesting people," she said.

Honk! Honk! came from a car before the Dutch door.

Walter lowered his newspaper. "But people are still in such a rush."

He walked to the compact and found a felt pen and some paper. Soon a sign hung in the front window of Toll 4. It read:

No rushing in this lane.
The Wilson Family

Around ten o'clock the traffic dwindled. Winona

closed the gate and joined her family on the patio.

"Who's up for a walk?" asked Walter. "It's time we

met our neighbors."

Together the four Wilsons crossed the lane to Toll 3.

At the door stood a woman of about thirty with long black

hair. Her toll-taker's hat sat far back on her head. Behind her a radio blared the morning news.

"Greetings, neighbor," said Walter. "We're the Wilsons, the toll takers next door."

The woman turned down her radio. "Thanks for stopping by," she said. "I'm Charlene. I don't get much company on this bridge."

At that moment, a green Buick stopped at the door, and the driver handed Charlene five one-dollar bills.

"Have a good day," she said.

"I see drivers give you money, too, Charlene," said Winona. "People who pass through this Toll Plaza are so kind."

Charlene's thin eyebrows crept up her forehead. "Gotta pay for this bridge somehow, honey," she said.

"You mean you're buying this bridge?" Winslow asked. "Fantabulous!"

"Bridges must be expensive," said Whitney.

"Once a man tried selling me the Brooklyn Bridge," Walter said. "But it was so old and dirty, I decided to pass."

Again Charlene's eyebrows rose. "Wise decision, honey. Now I better attend to my job. Have a good day."

The Wilsons waved and moved on to Toll 2.

Inside this cabin sat a man with a blond ponytail. He wore a jeans jacket and blue jeans. "Howdy, my name's Gene," he said. "You folks lost? Car trouble?"

"We're the Wilsons, and we're staying in Toll Four," said Walter.

Winona peered into the cabin. "Are you staying here by yourself?" she asked. "You must get lonely."

"Not at all," said Gene. "This is the only peaceful place I get to sit all day."

As he spoke the phone on the wall rang.

"But even on this bridge the peace and quiet doesn't last long," the man said, picking up the receiver. "I'll catch you folks later. I have to answer this call."

The Wilsons stepped to Toll 1. Behind this Dutch door sat a woman, who also had a blond ponytail. She also wore a jeans jacket and blue jeans and was also talking on the phone.

A little girl in denim overalls sat on the back shelf.

"Swimming! Swimming!" she shouted. "Ducks! Ducks!"

"Yes it is! No, I didn't!" the woman said into her phone. "I'm afraid you did! No, it isn't! Good-bye!"

She hung up the phone and addressed her visitors. "You must be the Wilsons. I'm Jean. My husband, Gene, said you were coming over."

Winona glanced back at Toll 2. "So you're married to Gene next door?" she asked.

"Gene and Jean. A pair of jeans," said Walter.

"Swimming! Swimming!" cried the toddler on the shelf. "Ducks! Ducks!"

The woman sighed and picked up the girl. "And this is our daughter Genie," she said. "She must have her father's genes. Very stubborn."

"I wanna go swimming!" the girl wailed. "I want to swim with the ducks."

"She also has a great pair of lungs," said Walter.

"I'm afraid Genie is a little ornery today," said Jean. "The terrible twos. She doesn't like coming to the Toll Plaza, but Gene and I couldn't find a sitter. I took her for the first hour. Now Gene is supposed to take her for the next hour, but he says he's too busy to come collect her."

"We'll walk Genie over for you," said Winona. "We're heading back that way."

"Oh, would you?" said Jean. "Neither Gene or I knew how much trouble having a two-year-old would be. We argue all the time."

"So that explains why they're staying in separate cabins," said Walter.

After saying good-bye to Jean, the Wilsons dropped Genie off with Gene in Toll 2. They passed Toll 3, waving to Charlene, and finally plopped into the lounge chairs outside Toll 4.

"What wonderful neighbors we have at this Toll Plaza," said Winona.

"Only the best," said Walter. "We must invite them over some evening for a game of bridge. *Ha! Ha!* Get it? Bridge on the bridge. *Ha! Ha! Haaa!*"

While Walter read the newspaper and Winona

sketched cars in her sketchbook, the twins went for a hike

on the sidewalk that ran along the side of the bridge. On

the way they found three hubcaps. Back at the cabin they

strung the shiny discs with fishing line and hung them from

the sunroof. When a breeze blew, the hub caps clanged

together and flashed in the sunlight.

"It's a modern art sculpture," Whitney explained.

"We're calling it *Hubcap Sunrise*," said Winslow.

"At least they should keep the crows away," said Walter.

Winona erased a line on her paper. "Oh, I wish the cars would stop long enough for me to draw them."

At that moment, a white convertible pulled up to the zebra-striped gate. The top was down, and a blond woman of about eighteen sat behind the wheel. Smoke poured from under the hood.

"Just what I need," the teenager said. "Car problems right in the middle of nowhere.

Winona set down her sketchbook. "You're never no where," she said to the girl. "Especially when you're here."

The girl climbed from the car, slamming the door. "Well, I'm stuck *here* wherever here is. My car's been smoking for the past ten miles."

"Smoking is a bad habit to get into, young lady" said Walter. "From the sound of your engine, you have a bad doohickey on the third thingamajig."

The teenager frowned. "Just what I need, car repair bills. I guess I'll hike into town and find a tow truck. And my name's not young lady; it's Faith."

"No need to go anywhere, Faith," said Walter. "I can fix that car in a jiffy."

"Walter loves tinkering with motors," Winona said. "Why don't you come sit down? I'll fix some lemonade, and we can chat while Walter tinkers."

The teenager shrugged. "Whatever," she said. "I wasn't heading anywhere anyway."

Walter rolled up his sleeves and approached the convertible. He popped opened the hood and leaned far over the engine. He hummed while he worked.

Meanwhile, Winona mixed lemonade in a plastic pitcher. She served a glass to Faith and the twins, and they sat in lounge chairs on the cement patio.

"So tell us about yourself, Faith," Winona asked. "Where are you from?"

Faith sipped from her glass. "There's not much to tell, really," she said.

"Faith's from New York," said Whitney. "I can see from her license plate."

"I *was* from New York," Faith said. "Now I'm driving out West to start a new life."

"A new life?" said Winona. "Aren't your parents worried about you?"

Faith shook her head. "My parents? They never care about anything I do. I doubt they even know I'm gone."

Walter stepped out from under the car hood. He held a small metal rod. "Here's the gizmo that broke off the whatchamacallit causing the thingamabob to smoke," he said. "I'll phone an auto shop and have a new doodad delivered to our Toll Plaza."

"Fantabulous! That means Faith can't go yet to wherever she was going," said Winslow.

"Hope you don't mind being stuck here in the middle of nowhere," said Whitney.

"Oh, I don't mind," the teenager said. "This rest is just what I needed. I've been driving all night."

Forty minutes later, a brown UPS van drove up to

the zebra-striped gate. A stocky woman in a brown shirt, shorts, and cap stepped out.

"Delivery for Toll Four," she said. "And I'm telling you, I've done hundreds of deliveries on either side of this bridge, but never one *on* the bridge.

Walter inspected the auto part the lady handed him. "Just the thingy I need," he said.

Clang! Clang! A breeze blew and stirred the hubcaps dangling under the sunroof.

"Isn't that beautiful?" said the UPS lady. "I'm telling you, this Toll Plaza has never looked lovelier."

"It's modern art," said Whitney.

"We call it *Hubcap Sensation*," Winslow said.

"And there's not a crow in sight," said Walter.

After the UPS truck left, another truck, this one

painted mustard yellow, drove onto the bridge. Words on

the side read:

**MOM'S JUST CHICKEN WAGON
GOOD LUNCHES AND DINNERS**

"Lunchtime," Walter said. "And you must stay for

lunch, Faith. The service at this Toll Plaza is excellent. I'll fix your car right after we eat"

The yellow van was heading toward Toll 2, but Walter waved it over to Toll 4.

The driver rolled down his window. He was an older man with a potbelly and thin gray hair. One sleeveless arm bore a tattoo of a chicken. "You open?" he asked.

"The Wilsons are always open for guests," said Walter.

"We were wondering if you were open," said Winona. "We'd like to have lunch on our patio."

The driver looked at Walter, Winona, Whitney, Winslow, and Faith. "Don't see why not," he said. "Business is business."

The man disappeared into the truck and seconds later a wide window on the side rolled up. The man stood behind a counter, wearing a paper apron and hat.

"It'll take a few minutes for the fryers to heat up," he said.

"Where's Mom?" asked Whitney.

"You're looking at him," said the man. "My real

name's Milton Oliver Montgomery. But friends call me Mom."

Walter drummed his finger on his large stomach. "So what's for lunch, Mom?"

"Chicken," came the answer. "Fried chicken, baked chicken, curried chicken, chicken kabobs, chicken nuggets, chicken burritos, chicken and dumplings, chicken pot pie, chicken fritters, or chicken on a stick. You name it, as long as it has chicken in it."

"How's business been?" asked Winona.

"Business is business," Mom repeated. "But to tell you the truth, I think my customers are getting tired of just chicken. To tell you the truth, I'm getting tired of cooking it."

At that moment, Huckleberry came strolling up the sidewalk. He held the bamboo pole in one hand and a string of large catfish in the other. When he reached the Toll Plaza his suntanned face broke out in a wide grin.

"What a morning of fishin', Wilsons," he said. "Walter, your marshmallow bait worked wonders. The second my hook touched the water a catfish attacked it. I caught enough fish for everyone."

Walter's eyes went from the fish to the lunch truck. "Mom, forget about cooking chicken for lunch," he said. "Let's have fresh catfish instead. I'll fry them myself, using our famous *Wilson Fish Batter* recipe."

Winona gave Walter a look. "I didn't know we had a famous *Wilson Fish Batter*," she said.

"It's so secret I'm the only Wilson who knows the ingredients," said Walter. "Is that all right with you Mom?"

"Anything other than chicken sounds all right with me," the man said.

As Huckleberry talked something behind him went "*Ruff! Ruff!*" The man stepped aside to reveal a scruffy gray dog. Its long eyebrows hid his eyes and his long mustache hid his mouth. "*Ruff! Ruff!*" he repeated.

"Who's your friend, Huck?" asked Walter.

"While I was fishin' this old pooch wandered up the bank, sniffin' at things," the man said. "Whenever a catfish fell off my hook, he pounced on it before it got away."

The dog wagged his long mop of a tail. *"Ruff! Ruff!"*

"Poor thing," said Faith. "He doesn't seem to have a home."

"I'm sure he's a stray," said Huckleberry.

"Then he can stay with us as long as he likes," said Walter.

Whitney pulled a hubcap off the sunroof and filled it with water. "And he can use this for a water dish."

"And I have a name for this fine pooch," said Walter. "Let's call him Bingo."

"B-I-N-G-O! B-I-N-G-O! B-I-N-G-O!" sang the twins. *"And Bingo is his name-o."*

"Welcome to the family, Bingo," said Winona.

"Ruff! Ruff!" went the dog.

At that moment Mom announced from the lunch truck, "The fat is ready for frying."

"Excellent," said Walter. "Time to whip up my secret batter."

"Whitney and Winslow, come help me clean these catfish," Huckleberry said.

"Faith and I will slice some potatoes," said Winona.

"We'll have catfish and French fries."

The group ate lunch in a circle on the patio. There was plenty of fish and fries for everyone.

"Fantabulous fish, Dad," said Winslow.

"Best fish I've ever had," Whitney agreed.

"Mmm, mmm," said Faith. "There's nothing like this in New York."

"*Ruff! Ruff!*" went Bingo, who had his share of catfish as well.

"What *did* you put in the *Wilson Fish Batter* to make the fish so crisp and fluffy, Walter?" asked Mom.

"Sorry my lips are sealed," Walter answered.

"*Ruff! Ruff!*" The dog now stood by the lunch wagon. In his mouth was an empty root beer can.

The group broke out laughing.

"Walter, you mixed *root beer* with flour, didn't you?" said Winona. "Root beer and flour is the secret *Wilson Fish Batter* recipe?"

"Bingo let the cat out of the bag," said Walter.

Mom wiped his hands on his apron. "Well, folks, I'm headed to the county fair across the river," he said.

"And if you don't mind, Walter, I'd like to try out your root-beer batter catfish on the crowd this evening."

"The recipe is all yours, Mom," Walter said. "Just change the name on your van to Mom's Chicken and Catfish Wagon.

Mom turned toward Huckleberry. "So what do you say, Huck? If you'll do the catchin', I'll do the cookin'. We'll split the profits fifty-fifty."

"If the Wilsons wouldn't mind taking over this toll cabin another day," Huck replied.

The four Wilsons were too busy eating catfish to do anything but nod.

Full of pep, promise, and the smell of catfish,

Mom and Huckleberry drove off in the lunch wagon to the county fair.

After Walter fixed Faith's car, Whitney said, "Let's go to the fair, too. Ferris wheels, farm animals, and fun houses."

"Ring toss games, roller-coasters, and rock n' roll,"

said Winslow.

"You youngsters go," said Walter. "The old folks will stay here and relax this afternoon."

Whitney grabbed Faith by one hand and Winslow took the other. Before the teenager could object, the twins pulled her to the convertible. The three sat in the front seat.

"Would you believe I've never been to a county fair before," Faith said. "This will be something new."

No sooner had the white convertible driven away, than the blast of police sirens shook the Toll Plaza. Ed, in his Illinois squad car, drove up to one side of the zebra-striped gate, while Fred on his Missouri police motorcycle roared up to the other. The two officers scowled at each other.

"*Ruff! Ruff!*" went Bingo.

"Greetings, officers," said Walter. "Nice of you fellows to drop by again."

Each policeman held up a picture of a girl. Underneath were the words:

TEENAGER MISSING
Name: Faith Harding

Home: New York, NY

"Either of you seen this girl?" Ed asked. "Her car's been spotted in Illinois."

"She's probably headed for Missouri by way of this bridge," said Fred.

Walter and Winona studied the picture. The face of Faith stared back at them.

Walter rubbed his chin. "So many people come and go around here," he said.

"Is this girl in trouble?" asked Winona.

"Faith Harding disappeared from her home three days ago," said Ed. "Her parents are worried silly about her."

"Probably just another runaway," said Fred. "If you see her, give a call to the Missouri State Police."

"Remember you're in Illinois now," said Ed. "So the Illinois State Police can handle this case best."

The policemen exchanged sour looks and returned to their vehicles. They made sharp U-turns, and sped away.

Walter gazed out at the river. "Now we know Faith

isn't driving toward a new life, but running away from her old one."

"Oh, Walter, what will we say to her when she gets back from the fair?" said Winona.

"We'll cross that bridge when we come to it," said Walter. "Right now it's a perfect time for a stroll across *our* bridge? Shall we?"

Winona took Walter by the arm. Together they started up the sidewalk. Bingo trotted at their heels.

The late afternoon was warm, and the smell of summer filled the air. The chocolaty Mississippi flowed beneath them without a ripple. Overhead, scissor-tailed swallows zipped in and out of the iron arches.

"*Bobby B. Bridges Memorial Bridge,*" Walter read off a sign. "Bobby B. Bridges must be the current owner of the bridge." He read another sign. "*No stopping on bridge. No diving from bridge. No passing on bridge. No throwing objects off bridge. No fishing from bridge.* Mr. Bridges doesn't seem to like having fun."

"Walter, I wonder why Faith ran away," said Winona. "Why did she say her parents don't care about her?"

"For emergency use only," Walter read off another sign. *"Speed zone ahead."*

"I just can't imagine anyone wanting to run away from their family," said Winona.

At the end of the bridge, the couple found FRANK'S FISHING BAIT AND FOOD MART. Inside they bought hamburger meat and buns for dinner.

"And here's the perfect dessert," said Walter, in the snack section. "Tollhouse cookies!"

Hand in hand, they started back to the Toll Plaza. By the time they arrived the sun had set, returning the sky to purple.

"Faith should be back with the twins any minute now," said Walter.

"But I still don't know what to say to her about Ed and Fred's visit," said Winona.

Walter bit into a cookie. "Not a thing. Our walk cleared my head. I now have a plan."

He entered Toll 4 and picked up the telephone. Winona watched him dial and chat to a mysterious someone. As he hung up the phone, car headlights lit up the cabin windows. A horn honked, and the white convertible pulled up to the gate.

Faith and Whitney sat in the front seat. Winslow sat in back with a giant stuffed panda. All three held clouds of cotton candy and were singing along with the radio.

Walter waved and joined Winona on the patio.

"What was that phone call about?" she asked him.

"A surprise," said Walter. "You'll have to wait until tomorrow night to see what it is."

Meanwhile, Faith and the twins had climbed from the car and ran back toward the Missouri shore, laughing and singing. There they raced up and down the riverbank catching fireflies. They put the blinking insects in a plastic bag, and back at the Toll Plaza, released them inside Toll 4. Soon the cabin was twinkling as much as both riverbanks and the sky above the bridge.

*H*onk! *Beep! Beep! Honk!*

Traffic woke the Wilsons again the next morning.

Walter sat up in his hammock. "That morning alarm does an excellent job," he said. "But it's hard to turn off."

Out the window, he spotted Faith curled up in the front seat of her car. For an instant the bear in back alarmed him, until he remembered Whitney had won it throwing darts at the county fair.

A newspaper plopped onto the patio, and the newspaperman waved to Walter.

"Good morning," Charlene called from Toll 3.

"Yes, another bracing morning on the bridge," Walter said. "Rise and shine, everyone!"

While the Wilsons rolled out of their hammocks, Faith appeared in the doorway. "I guess it's time to say good-bye," she said. "I guess I've been in your way long enough."

"Nonsense," said Winona. "There's plenty of room. You can stay as long as you like."

"You must come to our cookout tonight," said Walter. "We're inviting all our new friends and neighbors."

Faith smiled. "In that case, I guess I'll just drive into town and do some errands," she said. "See you later."

For breakfast, Walter grilled pancakes in the shape of famous buildings--the Eiffel Tower, the Gateway Arch, the Taj Mahal, and he surprised Winslow with a foot-long

Empire State Building pancake.

Afterwards, Winona placed a new sign in the toll cabin window:

WINONA'S ADVICE BOOTH
$5.00
HELP BUY THE BRIDGE

"Yesterday, drivers were eager to tell me their problems," she said. "This Rush Hour I'll accept their money in exchange for some sound Wilson wisdom."

Winona's first customer was a man in a white van. "I just had a fight with my daughter," he said. "She's in fourth grade, Winona. I feel bad that she went to school mad at me."

Winona leaned forward on her stool. "I understand your concern," she said. "But perhaps that's all water under the bridge by now. When your daughter comes home from school, make sure to listen to her, and I bet she's forgotten all about your argument."

The man's eyes lit up. "You think so, Winona? Maybe you're right. Maybe when Annie comes home she'll be eager to tell me all about her day as always." The man grinned as he handed Winona five dollars and drove away.

The next driver was a teenage girl in a blue Prius who thought school was a waste of time.

"I want to become a singer, Winona," she said. "So what's the point in studying math and science?"

Again Winona leaned forward. "Don't burn your bridges before you cross them, dear," she said.

The teenager nodded slowly. "Oh, wow! I think I know what you're saying, Winona. Wow! You're saying I should stay in school and practice my singing at the same time. That's what my parents say. Oh, wow! Awesome advice, Winona. Thanks."

That morning the sky was cloudless. By the time Rush Hour was over, the sun was baking the bridge. The Wilsons sat under the sunroof in swimsuits, fanning themselves with paper plates.

"It's too hot to hoot," said Walter. "But I see a way we can cool off."

A pickup truck had stopped next door. In back was a stack of inflated black inner tubes. Walter bought four tubes from the driver, and the Wilsons, inner tubes around their middles, climbed down the riverbank to the Mississippi River.

"*Ruff! Ruff!*" went Bingo, scampering after them.

Walter stuck a toe into the water. "Brrr. Forget it."

"Last one in is a river rat!" the twins cried, and they leaped right in. Their splashes soaked Walter, giving him no excuse not to jump in himself.

The current carried the Wilsons downstream at a lazy pace. They drifted under the bridge and past a boat marina.

"Greetings!" Walter called to an elderly couple on a houseboat. "Wonderful day to be on the river, isn't it?

"What a lovely, compact, floating house you have," said Winona.

A tugboat pushing three giant barges in the shape of cereal boxes, chugged past the family. *Phooot!* blasted its horn. The tugboat engine sent a high wave rolling toward them.

"Hold on, everyone," said Walter. "We're in for a ride."

Up and down, up and down went the inner tubes.

Up and down, up and down went the Wilsons.

"Yahoo!" Winslow cried

"Wheeeee!" shouted Whitney.

"I think I'm going to be sick," Walter moaned.

Farther downriver, the family floated up to a raft made of logs. A man wearing a straw hat and cut-off jeans sat on the edge, fishing.

No one recognized the fisherman until he pushed back his straw hat.

"Huckleberry!" the family chorused.

"How's the catfish business, Huck?" Walter asked

"Your root beer batter was a huge success at the fair," the former toll taker replied. "I reckon Mom's gonna need twice as many fish this evening. Yep, what can be better than sittin' and fishin' on the old Mississip?"

The Wilsons drifted on. The summer sun continued to beat down on them. While Winslow, Winona and Whitney wore T-shirts, Walter only had on his swim trunks. Already his round belly was as red as a raspberry.

"Walter, I think you should cover up a bit," said Winona.

"Nonsense," said Walter. "A little sun is good for you. Rich in vitamin-D."

Right then, merry calliope music drifted up the river.

"Sounds like a circus is coming!" said Whitney.

"Or a merry-go-round," said Winslow.

A minute later, a steam paddleboat appeared around the bend. Its four white decks, tiered like a birthday cake, gleamed in the sun. Ropes of steam rose from the twin smoke stacks. Printed on the side was THE MISSISSIPPI QUEEN, and in the rear, a big paddle wheel churned up the water.

As the boat passed the Wilsons, tourists leaned over the rails and waved. Whitney and Winslow pumped their fists in the air until *Phooooooooot!* The steam whistle bellowed, deep and loud.

"*That old man river!*" Walter sang. "*That old man river! He just keeps rolling along!*"

"Let's float all the way down to New Orleans," said Winslow.

"And across the ocean to Europe," said Whitney.

At this point Winona looked upstream. "Walter, we've floated a long way," she said. "I can't even see our bridge. How are we going to get back to the Toll Plaza?"

"No worry," Walter said. "Things have a way of working out for the Wilson family."

As he spoke, the Wilsons heard "*Ruff! Ruff!*" on the riverbank. Bingo and Faith stood on a boat ramp next to Faith's convertible.

"Need a lift?" Faith called out.

Arms and legs splashed the water, as the Wilsons paddled to shore. They loaded the inner tubes into Faith's trunk and piled into the car.

"Oooooo!" went Walter, sitting in back. His belly and shoulders were shiny red.

Faith pressed a button on the dashboard, and the convertible's top closed.

"Someone got a tad too much sun today," she said.

"Oooooo!" Walter repeated. "Yes, perhaps a tad too much vitamin D."

Back at Toll 4, the Wilsons and Faith prepared for

the party. Walter, careful not to let anything touch his

tender belly, poured charcoal in the grill. He sprinkled on

ample lighter fluid, tossed in a match, and *Phoom!* lit the

fire. Faith and the twins took charge of decorations and

entertainment. First, they drew wild designs on the cement

patio with colored chalk. Next, using strips of Walter's

newspaper, they made a long paper chain and strung it around the toll cabin. Finally, they sat in Faith's car to choose what music to play.

"We'll leave the car doors open and have an awesome sound system for dancing tonight," Faith said.

Meanwhile, Winona tidied up the little cabin. She dusted the shelves and washed the windows. While polishing the knob on the Dutch door, she watched Faith and the twins.

"Walter, doesn't Faith look much happier since coming here?" she said. "I'm worried what would happen if she leaves and continues west."

Walter shifted the coals in the grill. "Don't worry, my dear," he said. "This man has a plan."

"A plan?" said Winona.

"Tonight," said Walter.

A short while later, the brown UPS truck stopped at the gate. The woman in the brown uniform stepped out and handed Walter a box. "Here are the ribs you ordered, Mr. Wilson."

"Excellent timing, madam," said Walter. "And be

sure to come to our cook out tonight. We're having spareribs smothered in the famous *Wilson Barbecue Sauce*. It will be the best party west of the Mississippi, east of the Mississippi, and *above* the Mississippi."

Soon the sun set. Crickets chirped under the bridge and fireflies flashed on the riverbank.

"Our guests should arrive shortly," said Walter.

Charlene showed up first. Dressed in a blue party gown with her hair piled on top of her head, the Wilsons hardly recognized her. "I found a substitute to take over my toll cabin tonight," she said. "Someone has to collect those dollars."

Walter, who was wearing a mushroom chef's hat and an apron that said **KISS THE COOK**, dropped a sparerib on the grill. "I've grown as fond of this bridge as you, Charlene," he said. "If you don't buy it from Bobby B. Bridges, maybe I will."

Next Fred and Ed arrived with their wives Meg and Peg.

"I brought some ice cream for dessert," said Ned. "The state dessert of Missouri."

"And I brought some popcorn," said Ed. "State dessert of Illinois."

The UPS lady arrived wearing a brown dress followed by Mom, Huckleberry, and the newspaperman. Gene and Jean showed up with Genie between them.

"I wanna go swimming with the ducks!" the toddler screamed. "Swim! Swim! Ducks!"

Walter banged a dangling hubcap with his cooking fork. "Come and get it, folks," he called out. "The ribs are ready."

The meal was excellent. Besides barbecued ribs, the guests enjoyed fresh corn on the cob bought from a farmer who had driven through the Toll Plaza that afternoon, and a chocolate drink made by Winslow.

"I call it *Mississippi Mud*," he said.

For dessert, Whitney and Winslow amazed the crowd with their perfectly toasted marshmallows. Each time they lifted another golden one away from the coals the guests applauded. They served them pressed between two tollhouse cookies and a square of milk chocolate.

"Our new creation," said Winslow.

"We call them *Tollhouse S'mores*," said Whitney.

After dinner, Walter told a story about the Wilson's stay in New York City. "We loved the bright lights and friendly people," he said. "How lucky we were to stay in a small, cozy room right outside a Broadway theater. Not unlike Toll Four, it had windows on all sides. Many people came to visit at the front window, but they left when Winona told them the place was full."

Walter took a gulp of Mississippi Mud before continuing. "The next night we stayed in a room with one long window. It was in front of Macy's Department Store and was fully furnished. All evening we sat on the sofa, watching people stroll by on the sidewalk. Only the best for the Wilsons!"

As Walter talked, Winona watched Faith. The teenager sat alone on the hood of her car. She wore a yellow sundress and had stuck daisies in her hair.

"Your father's plans are always brilliant," she whispered to Whitney and Winslow. "But what has he cooked up this time that would prevent Faith from leaving tomorrow."

As she spoke, headlights lit up the patio. A yellow taxicab pulled up to the zebra-striped gate. From the rear seat emerged a middle-aged woman and man.

Faith gasped. Her hands went up to her mouth, and tears filled her eyes.

"Greetings and welcome to Toll Four," Walter said to the newcomers. "You must be Mr. and Mrs. Harding?"

"Harding?" Ed exclaimed. "Wasn't that the name of the missing girl on the Illinois State Police flyer?"

"The Missouri State Police have been looking for a Faith Harding all week," said Fred.

"Oh, Mom...Dad," Faith said. "What are you doing here?"

"Walter called us in New York," Mr. Harding said. "He told us our daughter was with his family."

"And you've come all this way to find me?" Faith asked.

"Faith, we were worried sick about you," said Mrs. Harding. "We've come to take you home with us."

"But I thought...," said Faith. And the next thing everyone at the party knew, the girl was wrapped in her parent's arms.

"*Ruff! Ruff!*" went Bingo.

At that moment the yellow parking lights on Faith's car came on, bathing the patio in a soft golden glow. Bouncy music sailed from the car speakers.

"Time for dancing!" Whitney called from the front seat.

Walter threw off his cook's apron and grabbed Winona by the hand. "Let's cut the rug, Winona," he said. And they began dancing cheek to cheek in the middle of the patio.

Other couples joined them--Gene and Jean, Fred and Meg, Ed and Peg, Huckleberry and the UPS lady, Charlene and Mom, Mr. and Mrs. Harding, Faith and Winslow, and Whitney danced with the stuffed panda.

"Walter, you did it again," said Winona. "Your surprise was a brilliant prize for Faith."

Walter twirled Winona under his arm. "Only the best," he said.

Not until past midnight did the first guests leave. Mr. and Mrs. Harding drove off with Faith in her convertible. One by one the other partygoers drove toward Illinois or Missouri. They all agree it was the best party west of the Mississippi, east of the Mississippi, and *above* the Mississippi.

By the time Winona opened the zebra-striped gate

the next morning, a line of twenty cars had formed outside

the Dutch door. Word had traveled quickly about

Winona's Advice Booth, and she was in great demand.

As Winona talked to drivers, Walter and the twins

lounged on the patio, reading the newspaper and

paperback books.

"I'm reading a book about the Rocky Mountains," said Winslow. "Did you know that ski areas have little cabins that move up and down the side of mountains on wires?"

"Excellent," said Walter. "We'll put that on the Wilson's Bucket List of places to stay."

"*Ruff! Ruff!*" went Bingo.

"I'm reading *The Little House in the Big Woods*," said Whitney.

"Ah, the good old days," said Walter.

At that moment the phone inside the small cabin rang. Walter rose to answer it.

"*Hello, Walter,*" said a voice. "*This is Gene in Number Two.*"

Walter looked out the window and gave the thumbs up sign. "What can I do for you, Gene?"

"*Walter, I'm worried about Jean and Genie,*" Gene said. "*They went for a walk along the river this morning and were supposed to be at the Toll Plaza by nine. Could you check if you can spot them off your side of the bridge?*"

"Just a sec, Gene," said Walter. He hustled to the compact and took a pair of binoculars from the glove compartment. Leaning over the bridge railing, he scanned the riverbank.

Back on the phone he reported, "No luck, Gene. I see only the usual fishermen and joggers."

A few minutes later, Ed on his motorcycle and Fred in his squad car drove up to Toll 2. With the Wilsons watching, Gene closed his gate, and drove off with Fred.

"Doesn't look good," said Walter.

"I'm telling all my customers to keep an eye out for Jean and Genie," said Winona.

Again the phone rang, and Walter answered it. It was Charlene. *"Have you heard the news?"* she said. *"Gene found Jean, but Genie's still missing. Ed and Fred have organized two search parties on both sides of the Mississippi."*

Walter hung up, looking grim. "We have an emergency, family," he said to the others. "Little Genie has vanished."

Whitney lowered her paperback. "Yesterday, Genie had one thing on her mind," she said.

"Last night that's all she talked about," said Winona.

"Swimming with the ducks," the Wilsons said together.

Again Walter held the binoculars to his eyes. This time instead of searching the riverbanks, he checked the river. Almost at once, he spotted something in the water. A blue plastic trash barrel, floating on end, was drifting toward the bridge. Walter focused the lenses. Yes, inside the barrel stood a small figure. Genie. The girl appeared unharmed, but the barrel was wobbling, and the smallest wave would topple it over.

"I'll call 911," said Winona, reaching for the phone.

"No time," said Winslow.

"We must rescue Genie ourselves," said Whitney.

"Quick, grab your inner tubes!" Walter called out. "Wilsons to the rescue!"

W ithin a minute, the four Wilsons were charging

down the riverbank, rolling the inner tubes before them.

About fifty yards upriver, the blue barrel bobbed in

the water. Genie's head appeared over the top. Even

from this distance the Wilsons heard her wailing, "Swim!

Swim! Swim! Ducks! Ducks!"

Walter stood on the water's edge. "The little tike sounds as healthy as ever," he said.

"If we paddle straight out, I think we can reach her before she floats by," said Winona.

With inner tubes around their middles, the Wilsons leaped into the river. By the time they reached midstream, they were directly under the bridge. The blue barrel drifted toward them, less than ten yards away.

Genie waved her arms, screaming, "Swim! Swim! Quack! Quack!"

All at once the barrel tipped. The toddler plunged into the water face first.

"I got her," Walter said, and he vanished underwater.

For several silent seconds, the Mississippi River seemed to stand still.

"Where are they?" called Winona.

"I can't see them," said Whitney.

"How long can Dad stay under?" said Winslow.

Like two fishing bobbers, Walter and Genie's heads popped to the surface. Holding the toddler by the armpits,

Walter heaved her onto his inner tube.

The girl clapped her hands and giggled. "I was swimming! I was swimming like a duck!"

Walter spit out some water "You sank like a stone, kid," he sputtered.

With Genie perched on the front of Walter's inner tube, the Wilsons swam for shore.

Jean and Gene were standing there to greet them. The instant Genie was within arm's reach, they lifted her off the tube and smothered her with hugs and kisses.

"Genie and I were sitting on the riverbank, watching ducks," Jean explained. "When I turned, she was gone."

"We saw the whole rescue from the bridge, Walter," Gene said.

"I wanna swim again," Genie said. "I wanna swim like a duck!"

At that moment a van with a large 11 on its side stopped on the bridge. A man carrying a TV camera on his shoulder and a woman holding a microphone ran down the riverbank.

"We're , *live*, all *live* on the banks of the Mississippi

River," the woman said into her mic. "Seconds ago, a family floating in inner tubes, pulled a small girl, *alive*, out of the river under the Billy Bob Bridges Memorial Bridge."

The woman pushed her microphone toward the Wilsons who were patting themselves dry with towels.

"We're *live* on Channel Eleven News," she said. "Please tell the world your names. Where are you from?"

"We're the Wilsons," said Walter.

"And we're staying at the Toll Plaza," said Winona.

The news reporter's eyes widened. "The Wilsons?" she said. "Aren't you the famous family who stayed in an elevator at the San Francisco Hotel? The newspaper called you the *Elevator Family!*"

"That vacation was fantabulous," said Winslow.

"It had its ups and downs," said Whitney.

When the Wilsons returned to Toll 4, the phone didn't stop ringing. Car after car stopped at the Dutch door, carrying people who wanted autographs and pictures of the Elevator Family. Again and again the UPS lady drove up to deliver gifts and flowers.

Mom parked his lunch wagon next to the patio.

"Business is business," he said, and he began selling catfish fried in *Wilson Fish Batter*. All afternoon Huckleberry raced up and down the riverbank, bringing more fish.

Around six that evening the governors of Missouri and Illinois appeared at the Toll Plaza. Both were short white-haired men who wore white suits.

"Greetings Walter, Winona, Winslow and Whitney," the Missouri governor said.

"Hello, Wilson family," said Illinois's governor.

"Until today this bridge has been called the Bobby B. Bridges Memorial Bridge," said the first governor.

"But frankly no one in either of our state governments can remember who Bobby Bridges was," said the second governor.

"So in honor of this historic occasion," Missouri's governor went on, "we have both agreed to rename the bridge in your honor."

" From now on, Walter, Winona, Winslow, and Whitney," said Illinois's governor. "This bridge will be called...."

"*The Elevator Family Bridge*," the governors said

together.

The Wilson's final evening at Toll 4 was not as peaceful as they had planned. The zebra-striped gate remained raised and a stream of reporters and tourists drove by to meet the famous family.

"Guests are always welcome at our home," Walter said to every one who came.

*H*onk! *Honk! Beep! Beep! Varooom!*

The next morning the four Wilsons rose early and took down their hammocks.

With a nod, Walter removed the **HOME SWEAT HOME** sampler from the wall. "Until the next excellent place we stay," he said.

While the twins pulled down the hubcap sculpture and party decorations, Winona posted a new sign in the window:

SORRY CHECKED OUT

"I've talked to the other toll takers," she said. "They've agreed to listen to any commuter who needs to talk during Rush Hour."

The newspaperman drove by, shouting, "Extra! Extra! Read all about yourselves, Wilsons!"

Walter picked up the newspaper that plopped on the patio and smiled at the picture of his family on the front page. The headlines read:

LOCAL "DUCK" GIRL SAVED
BY ELEVATOR FAMILY.

"Another page for the family scrapbook," he said.

After sweeping out the little cabin and patio, the Wilsons piled into the green compact.

Bingo sat on the curb. *"Ruff! Ruff!"*

"Come on, boy," said Whitney. "Hop in!"

"You're a member of the family now," said Winslow. "We have your hubcap water dish all packed."

The dog sprang toward the car. He bounded into the back seat next to the twins and the giant panda.

As Walter revved up the motor, Faith's white convertible pulled up to the gate. Faith was driving and her parents sat in back.

"We read about the Elevator Family in the morning paper," Mrs. Harding called out. "Bravo!"

"We're taking Faith back to New York with us," said Mr. Harding. "We stopped by to thank your family for getting *our* family back together."

"And what will you be doing in New York, Faith?" asked Winona.

"That's another thing I have to thank the Wilsons for," said Faith. "You see, while I was staying on this bridge I studied it closely. I marveled at the overhead girders and arches. It's like a giant puzzle joined together with bolts. My father told me civil engineers design bridges, so next fall I'll start studying civil engineering at the university."

"Excellent choice," said Walter.

"Maybe someday we'll stay on a bridge built by Faith Harding," said Winona.

With a wave of hands, the Hardings drove off. By now Rush Hour had started. Gene, Jean, and Charlene were busy taking money from morning commuters.

Walter steered the compact over to Charlene's Dutch door. He held out a five-dollar bill.

"Here's a small contribution to your Bridge-Buying Fund, Charlene," he said.

Charlene pushed her hat far back on her head. "Farewell, Wilsons. I'll miss you at this Toll Plaza," she said. "Since you came here, drivers have never been more friendly."

"And we hope our friendship bridges a lifetime, Charlene," said Winona.

"Westward-ho!" the twins called out, and the green compact started down the highway again.

"*Ruff! Ruff!*" went Bingo.

As Walter, Winona, Winslow, and Whitney crossed the bridge, now *The Elevator Family Bridge*, they broke out in a song,

> *"There was a family, who has a dog,*
> *And Bingo is his name-o!*
> *B-I-N-G-O! B-I-N-G-O! B-I-N-G-O!*
> *And Bingo is his name-o!"*

Made in the USA
Lexington, KY
21 December 2014